How to
be a
Flower
Fairy

FREDERICK WARNE

Published by the Penguin Group
Penguin Books Ltd, 80 Strand, London WC2R 0RL, England
Penguin Young Readers Group, 345 Hudson Street, New York, New York 10014, U.S.A
Penguin Books Australia Ltd, 250 Camberwell Road,
Camberwell, Victoria 3124, Australia
Penguin Books Canada Ltd, 10 Alcorn Avenue,
Toronto, Ontario, Canada M4V 3B2
Penguin Group (NZ), Cnr Airborne and Rosedale Roads,
Albany, Auckland 1310, New Zealand
Penguin Books India (P) Ltd, 11 Community Centre,
Panchsheel Park, New Delhi 110 017, India
Penguin Books (South Africa) (Pty) Ltd, PO Box 9, Parklands 2121, South Africa
Penguin Books Ltd, Registered Offices: 80 Strand, London WC2R 0RL, England

Website at: www.flowerfairies.com

First published by Frederick Warne 2004
Copyright © Frederick Warne & Co., 2004
Original illustrations copyright © The Estate of Cicely Mary Barker,
1923, 1925, 1926, 1934, 1940, 1944, 1948
New reproductions copyright © The Estate of Cicely Mary Barker, 1990

Based upon 'How to be a Flower Fairy' published
by Frederick Warne in 2000

ISBN 0-7232-4993-8

Printed in China

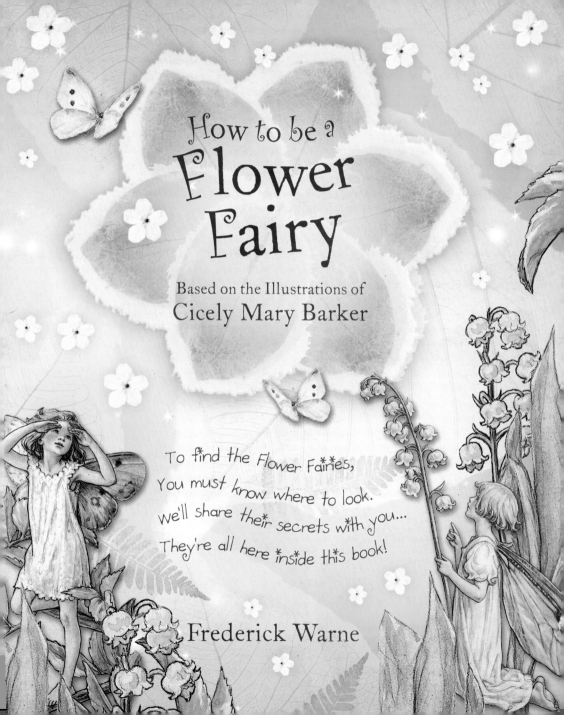

How to be a
Flower
Fairy

Based on the Illustrations of
Cicely Mary Barker

To find the Flower Fairies,
You must know where to look.
We'll share their secrets with you...
They're all here inside this book!

Frederick Warne

Welcome to Flower Fairy Land!

The Flower Fairies' land is filled with
hidden treasures and surprises! To become
a Flower Fairy, recite this enchanted rhyme:

"I close my eyes and count to five
To make the fairies come alive.
And when I open them, I see
There is a brand new fairy – me!"

Now you've taken the first step to becoming a Flower Fairy, take a little fairy peek inside this flowery pocket and see what secrets you can discover...

Flower Fairy Friends

In this lively world, every fairy is your friend. But it's nice to have someone special to play with. Follow the trail of leaves and answer the questions to find your very own Flower Fairy friend!

Start

Do you love summer best of all?

yes

no

Do you like the colour pink?

n

Are you mischievous?

ye.

no

Do you like playing in the garden?

no

yes

es

es

Do you
like fruit?

yes

no

yes

Do you
like autumn?

no

Is your favourite
colour lilac?

yes

no

The World Outside

Every Flower Fairy knows the plants and animals they share their world with. If you have a garden, explore it in every season, or just keep your eyes open when you're outside. You never know what you'll find!

Try to spot these seasonal flowers and berries!

Summer:
Daisies
Roses

Spring:
Daffodils
Crocuses

Winter:
Winter Jasmine
Snowdrops

Autumn:
Elderberry
Blackberry

The Flower Fairies are good friends with lots of animals too. Have you ever seen a:

Butterfly   Rabbit   Spider   Squirrel
Grasshopper   Snail   Bee

Flower Keepsake

Flowers look beautiful when they are growing outside, but pressed flowers are lovely too. Always ask an adult before you pick any flowers.

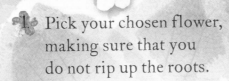

1. Pick your chosen flower, making sure that you do not rip up the roots.

2. Let it dry out at home for a day or two.

3. Place your flower between the pages of a notebook, then place a heavy book on top so that it is flattened.

4. Leave in a dry place for about a week and then open up the notebook.

Why not glue your flower to some paper and put it in a picture frame?

Secret Flower Fairy Codes

Flower Fairies love to keep in touch with each other.
Why not write to your friends using the leaf-shaped
postcards on the page opposite? Try writing in either the
Flower Fairy code below (making sure your friends have
a copy of the code!) or in secret ink.

Secret Fairy Code

a🍎 b🐝 c◎ d✧ e❉ f🌷 g❖ h♥ i○
j🌸 k➹ l: m☽ n□ o🌷 p🦀 q★ r△
s☆ t+ u✳ v♡ w❄ x🦋 y✕ z🌿

Iris has written Herb Twopence a letter using the
secret fairy alphabet. Can you work out what it says?

Spellbinding Secret Ink

To start, mix together equal amounts of
salt and warm water. Two spoonfuls of each
should be enough.

1. Dip a thin paintbrush in the magic mixture and draw
   or write a message or picture on a piece of white paper.

2. Let it dry. When it has dried completely,
   your message will be invisible!

3. Send your message.

4. To see the message, rub your
   pencil gently over the area.

Flower Fairy Tip:
Make sure the friend you
    are writing to knows
       how to make the
          message visible!

Dressing For The Fairy Ball

The fairy ball is a very special event. The Fairies polish their wings until they sparkle, and wear beautiful jewels. To make your own bracelet, crown and necklace, look under these flaps. Then put on the wings inside this pack. Now you're ready for the ball!

White Briony says: For even more fairy sparkle, add some extra beads to your charm bracelet!

Fairy Charm Bracelet

Every fairy has their own special charm, and now you have your own, too! Push out these charms and thread string through the holes. Then tie it to your wrist in a pretty bow.

Your crown
will look just like the one
Guelder Rose is wearing!

Crown and Necklace

The larger flowers inside this envelope are for your crown, and the smaller flowers are for your necklace. Push out the flower shapes and thread string through the holes. Ask an adult to tie the crown around your head, and the necklace around your neck.

Make sure that the crown fits snugly around the top of your head, and the necklace fits loosely around your neck.

Magic Fairy Spells!

Spells are an important part of the Flower Fairies' world. And although there are a mixture of naughty and nice fairies in the fairy world, they always use their magic powers to do good.

The Sunshine Spell

To bring out the sun, make a chain of buttercups and wear them in your hair. Spin around three times and repeat this rhyme...

'Glitter, glimmer magic sun, shine your light on everyone!'

The Birthday Spell

When it's your birthday, make a wish while planting seeds. Your wish should grow with your plant!

'Pretty plant I do love you, please grow and make my wish come true!'

The Rain Spell

Take a cup of water and add a few blades of grass. Using a twig, stir three times to the left and three times to the right, then pour the potion onto the roots of the tree. It should soon rain!

'Pitter, patter, drops of rain, feed the garden once again!'

A Place for Fairy Thoughts!

All Flower Fairies have a special notebook where they write down their thoughts. Look on the page opposite for your own fairy notebook! To see the sort of things Flower Fairies write about, take a peek at the pages of Wild Rose's and Horse Chestnut's notepads.

Here are some of the things that you could write in your notebook:

- The names of your best friends.
- Special birthdays and occasions.
- Your favourite fairy words!

Today I had a lovely time tending to my blooms in the Summer sunshine. Tomorrow I must remember to wake up with the

first rays of the sun so I can polish my leaves with morning dew, until they sparkle and shine. I want to make sure I l my best for the Fairy Summer ball!

At Fairy school today I got into trouble for dropping some of my burrs and disrupting the wishing class. I've promised to be good from now on!

Things to do:

* Write Acorn a special birthday poem.

* Ask Pink to help me sew up my tunic.

* Practise my wishes!

Fairy Market Day

Every month the Flower Fairies hold a market. They sell delicious fruit, clothes sewn from petals and beautiful jewels! What will you buy from the Fairy market?

Sweet fruit

All the sweetest berries of the seasons are for sale!

Cups and bowls

Dainty dishes are created from buds and leaves.

Delicate Shoes

Shoes are sewn from petals,
with a touch of added fairy dust!

Sparkly Stickers

Decorate paper and notebooks
with these fairy stickers!

Beautiful Gowns

Tansy spends days sewing
stunning outfits to sell.

Enter, Flower Fairies!

You can't live outside with the Flower Fairies, but you can make sure that everyone knows that they are entering into a fairy world when they approach your room!

Enchanted Door Sign

You will need:

- blunt-ended scissors
- coloured pens
- thick paper
- tape
- pretty things to decorate!

Always ask an adult to help you with cutting out.

1. Take a piece of thick paper or card and fold it in half.

2. Draw the petals of a flower sprouting out of the folded edge. See diagram.

3. Cut around the edge of the petals. When you open out the card you'll have a flower shape.

4. Write the following words on the sign:

You are about to enter the secret fairy den of....... (space for your name). Only friends of the Flower Fairies allowed!

5. Decorate your sign. Add beads or sequins, or stick on some pressed flowers. Draw pictures of Flower Fairies, attach these to some ribbon or string, and then hang these from the back of your sign.

You are about to enter the secret fairy den of Cassie!

Goodnight, Flower Fairies!

Every Flower Fairy needs a good night's sleep to be at their very best! To sleep like a fairy, why not try these two flower remedies? Remember to always ask an adult before picking any flowers.

Scented Bathing

Sometimes there's nothing better than a bath before bed to send you right off to sleep!

1. Get permission to pick some flowers and leave them to dry for a few days in a warm place.

2. Carefully pluck the petals from the flower.

3. Ask an adult to help you run a nice warm bath, and add a little bath oil. Scatter the petals over the surface of the bath, and enjoy!

Lovely Lavender

1. Cut a bunch of flowering lavender and stand in a vase without water. It will smell delicious and should take just a few days to dry out naturally.

2. Remove the lavender stalks, take a handkerchief and put a handful of lavender in the middle.

3. Gather the sides together and tie with a pretty ribbon. Then store it with your bed linen or put under your pillow.

4. The soothing scent of lavender will soon help you drift off to sleep!

Sleep Tight Fairy Rhyme:

"Say goodbye to this precious day,
It's been full of magic, fun and play!
It's time for the fairies to bid you goodnight,
Have sweet dreams, we hope you sleep tight!"

Fairy Farewell

Now you know how to be a Flower Fairy! We hope that you've enjoyed this book and have learned lots about the way we live. We are looking forward to seeing you soon, so make sure you keep your eyes open for us!
Love,
the Flower Fairies
xx